Dear Parents,

Welcome to the Scholastic Reader series. We have taken over 80 years of experience with teachers, parents, and children and put it into a program that is designed to match your child's interests and skills.

Level 1—Short sentences and stories made up of words kids can sound out using their phonics skills and words that are important to remember.

Level 2—Longer sentences and stories with words kids need to know and new "big" words that they will want to know.

Level 3—From sentences to paragraphs to longer stories, these books have large "chunks" of texts and are made up of a rich vocabulary.

Level 4—First chapter books with more words and fewer pictures.

It is important that children learn to read well enough to succeed in school and beyond. Here are ideas for reading this book with your child:

- Look at the book together. Encourage your child to read the title and make a prediction about the story.
- Read the book together. Encourage your child to sound out words when appropriate. When your child struggles, you can help by providing the word.
- Encourage your child to retell the story. This is a great way to check for comprehension.
- Have your child take the fluency test on the last page to check progress.

Scholastic Readers are designed to support your child's efforts to learn how to read at every age and every stage. Enjoy helping your child learn to read and love to read.

      —**Francie Alexander**
      Chief Education Officer
      Scholastic Education

Copyright © 2001 by Norman Bridwell.
Activities copyright © 2003 Scholastic Inc.
All rights reserved. Published by Scholastic Inc.
SCHOLASTIC, CARTWHEEL BOOKS, and associated logos
are trademarks and/or registered trademarks of Scholastic Inc.
CLIFFORD, CLIFFORD THE BIG RED DOG, and associated logos are
trademarks and/or registered trademarks of Norman Bridwell.

Library of Congress Cataloging-in-Publication Data is available.

ISBN: 0-439-18300-6

20 19 18 17 16 15 14   04 05
Printed in the U.S.A. 23 • First printing, January 2001

Norman Bridwell

CLIFFORD'S®

VALENTINES

Scholastic Reader — Level 1

SCHOLASTIC INC.

Cartwheel
K·S·®

New York   Toronto   London   Auckland   Sydney
Mexico City   New Delhi   Hong Kong   Buenos Aires

It is Valentine's Day.

Clifford gets a card.
It is from a boy.

Clifford gets a card.
It is from a girl.

Clifford gets a card
from a woman.

Clifford gets a card
from a man.

The letter carrier comes.

Now Clifford gets many, many more cards.
Everyone loves Clifford!

It starts to snow.

It snows and snows.
Clifford has an idea.

He runs to the park.

The boy, the girl, the woman,
and the man are there.

Many, many other people are there, too.

Clifford makes a heart in the snow.

Happy Valentine's Day, everyone!

• Word List •

a	it
an	letter
and	loves
are	makes
boy	man
card	many
carrier	more
Clifford	now
comes	other
day	park
everyone	people
from	runs
gets	snow
girl	starts
happy	the
has	there
heart	to
idea	too
in	Valentine's
is	woman